Paddington Bear
in the Garden

MICHAEL BOND   Pictures by R. W. ALLEY

HarperCollins*Publishers*

Paddington Bear in the Garden

Text copyright © 2002 by Michael Bond. Illustrations copyright © 2002 by R. W. Alley. First published in Great Britain by Collins in 2001. Collins is an imprint of HarperCollins Publishers Ltd. First American Edition 2002. Manufactured in China. All rights reserved. Library of Congress card number 2001088439 www.harperchildrens.com

One morning Paddington took some paper and a pencil into the garden and began making a list of all the nice things he could think of about being a bear and living with the Browns.

To start with, he had a room of his own and a warm bed to sleep in. And he had marmalade for breakfast *every* morning. In Darkest Peru he had only been allowed it on Sundays.

The list grew longer and longer, and he had nearly run out of paper before he realized he had left out one of the nicest things of all . . .

 . . . the garden!

Paddington liked the Browns' garden. Apart from the occasional noise from a nearby building site, it was so quiet and peaceful it didn't seem like being in London at all.

But nice gardens don't just happen. They usually require a lot of hard work, and the one at number thirty-two Windsor Gardens was no exception. Mr. Brown had to mow the lawn twice a week, and Mrs. Brown was kept busy weeding the flower beds. There was always something to do. Even Mrs. Bird lent a hand whenever she had a spare moment.

It was Mrs. Bird who first suggested giving Jonathan, Judy, and Paddington each a piece of the garden.

"It will keep certain bears out of mischief," she said meaningly. "And it'll help you both at the same time."

Mr. Brown agreed it was a very good idea, and he measured out three plots at the far end of the lawn.

Paddington was most excited. "I don't suppose there are many bears who have their own garden!" he exclaimed.

Early the next morning all three set to work.

Judy decided to make a flower bed, and Jonathan had

his eye on some old paving stones, but Paddington didn't

know what to do. In the past he

had often found that gardening

was much harder work than it

looked, especially when you only

had paws.

In the end, armed with a jar of Mrs. Bird's homemade marmalade, he borrowed Mr. Brown's wheelbarrow and set off to look for ideas.

His first stop was a booth in the market, and there he bought a book called *How to Plan Your Garden* by Lionel Trug.

The book came complete with a large packet of assorted seeds, and if the picture on the front cover was anything to go by, gardening must be very relaxing. Mr. Trug seemed to do most of his planning while lying in a hammock. By the end of the book, without lifting a finger, he was surrounded by blooms of every possible size and color.

Paddington decided it was a very good value indeed— especially when the owner of the booth gave him two pence change.

Mr. Trug's book was full of useful hints and tips, and Paddington couldn't wait to try some of them out.

The very first tip suggested that before starting work it was a good idea to close your eyes and try to picture what the garden would look like when it was finished.

Having walked into a lamppost by mistake, Paddington decided to read another page or two, and there he found a much better idea. Mr. Trug advised standing back and looking at the site from a safe distance, preferably somewhere high up.

He knew just the spot.

By the time Paddington reached the building site near the Browns' house, it was the middle of the morning and the men were all at their tea break.

Placing his jar of marmalade on a wooden platform for safekeeping, he sat on a pile of bricks for a rest while he considered the matter.

There was no one around. . . .

And there was a ladder nearby. . . .

Mr. Trug was quite right. The Browns' garden did look very different from high up. Judy was digging away at her patch of ground, and not far away Jonathan was trying to break a paving stone in two.

Just then Paddington heard the sound of an engine starting, and, standing well back in case Mrs. Bird saw him, he peered through a gap in the boards. As he did so, his eyes nearly popped out.

On the ground just below him, a man was emptying a load of concrete on the very spot where he had left his jar of marmalade!

Paddington scrambled back down the ladder as fast as his legs would carry him, reaching the bottom just as the foreman came around a corner.

"Is anything wrong?" asked the man. "You look upset."

"My jar's been buried!" exclaimed Paddington hotly, pointing to the pile of concrete. "It had some of Mrs. Bird's best golden chunks in it, too!"

The foreman called his men together. "There's a young bear gentleman here who's lost some very valuable chunks," he said urgently. "Better get cracking."

"I won't ask how your jar got there," he said, turning to Paddington as the men set to work clearing the concrete into small piles, "or what you were doing up the ladder."

"I'm glad of that," said Paddington, politely raising his hat.

Suddenly there was a whirring sound from somewhere overhead, and, to Paddington's surprise, the platform landed at his feet. "My marmalade!" he exclaimed thankfully.

"Your marmalade?" repeated the foreman, staring at the jar. "Did you say marmalade?"

"That's right," said Paddington. "I put it there ready for my elevenses. It must have been taken up by mistake. Now the top's come off!"

It was the foreman's turn to look as though he could hardly believe his eyes.

"That's special quick-drying cement!" he wailed. "It's probably rock-hard already—ruined by a bear's marmalade! No one will give me two pence for it now!"

"I will," said Paddington eagerly.

"I've had an idea!"

It took Paddington several trips to take all the lumps of concrete home in the wheelbarrow, and it kept him busy for most of the week.

When the builders saw the rock garden he had made, they were most impressed, and the foreman even gave Paddington some plants to finish it off until his seeds started to grow.

"It's National Garden Day on Saturday," he said. "There are some very famous people judging it. I'll spread the word around. You never know your luck."

The foreman was as good as his word, and on Saturday half the neighborhood turned up at number thirty-two Windsor Gardens to see the judges arrive.

Paddington nearly fell over backward in surprise when he discovered that no less a person than Mr. Lionel Trug himself was leading the procession.

"It's very good of you to get out
of your hammock, Mr. Trug!" he exclaimed.

"Er . . . not at all," said Lionel Trug.
"My pleasure. I must say, I love your
orange stones. Where did you find
them?"

"I didn't," said Paddington.
"I think they found me.
Thanks to the builders."

"Congratulations!" said Mr. Trug, as he handed Paddington a gold star. "It's good to see a young bear taking up gardening. I hope you will be the first of many." And to show how pleased he was, he gave both Jonathan and Judy a silver medal so that they wouldn't feel left out.

"Who would have believed it?" said Mr. Brown, as the last of the crowd departed.

"You must write and tell Aunt Lucy all about it," said Mrs. Bird. "They'll be very excited in the Home for Retired Bears when they hear the news."

Paddington thought that was a good idea, but he had something to do first.

He wanted to add one more important item to his list of all the nice things there were about being a bear and living with the Browns:

HAVING MY OWN ROCK GARDEN!

Then he signed his name and added his special paw print . . .

. . . just to show it was genuine.